To Poppa V
Music is all around us. I was lucky enough
to have a father who helped me hear it. —CAFV

To my Mama and Papa,
Thank you for believing in me and not forcing me
to become a dentist. —LC

THE OBOE GOES BOOM BOOM BOOM

BY **COLLEEN AF VENABLE**
PICTURES BY **LIAN CHO**

GREENWILLOW BOOKS

An Imprint of HarperCollins Publishers

It's time!
Are you excited?
I bet you are, because today you are joining . . .

THE BAND!

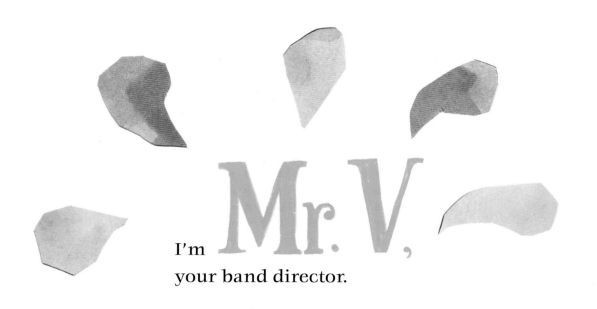

I'm **Mr. V,**
your band director.

There is a perfect instrument for everyone.

Let's find yours!

You could play the

Clarinet.

Clarinets are part of the

WOODWIND

family.

See this tiny stick?

It may look like it belongs in a Popsicle, but it's actually

SCIENCE.

We call it a "reed."

That's me!

That's not me!

When you blow on it, it

WIGGLES

back and forth and back and forth and all that wiggling produces a musical note. The harder you blow, the faster the reed vibrates and the louder the sound.

But be careful.

If you blow TOO hard, the clarinet will squeak and mice will fall in love with you.

I'm kidding! *

* That's only happened once.

Listening to a clarinet is like eating rich chocolate cake,

BOLD and Sweet

at the same time.

Sid, are you ready to demonstrate?

The clarinet goes . . .

Felicity, I'm glad you're excited, but please wait your turn. I'll talk about the drums soon. But first, let me tell you about the . . .

Trumpet!

A trumpet is part of the brass family. Armies used to charge into battle to the sound of triumphant trumpet toots!

toot toot toot toot toot toot toot toot toot toot

Heh heh toot toot

Stop that giggling, Val. Not *those* kind of toots.

The trumpet has only three buttons, or valves.

1
2
3

So how can a trumpet play more than three notes?

Two ways!

Trumpets are made of a series of tubes that *twist and turn.*

When you press down the valves, they work like gates, closing off channels to make the airflow shorter or longer, and that creates higher or lower notes.

If you unraveled a trumpet's coils, it would be five feet tall!

The other way to make different notes is with your lips. Hold your lips loose, blow, and make a funny sound like a grumpy horse.

Now tighten your lips and try to make the same sound. When you hold your mouth tight and play the trumpet, your lips vibrate faster, and the faster vibrations make higher notes! (And often very funny faces.)

Trumpets have a sharp, crisp sound, like the crunch of an apple.

The trumpet goes . . .

Felicity!
Please get back to your spot.

Want to play something rare? How about the

OBOe?

Like the clarinet, the oboe is a woodwind, but compared to the rows of clarinet players in the band, our oboe player—like the cheese in a nursery rhyme—stands alone.

It's just a figure of speech, Widdy. You can sit down.

Instead of 1 reed, an oboe uses 2.

They *Vibrate* against each other, creating an entirely new sound. It's one of the hardest instruments to master.

When you start playing, it WILL sound like an angry duck who landed on an icy lake.

But play it right and that duck will learn to ice skate and glide its way to Olympic gold.

Widdy, are you ready?

The oboe goes . . .

**FELICITY!
WAIT YOUR TURN!**

There's always the **Flute.**

Another member of the woodwind
family, the flute is one of the oldest
instruments in the world.
How long has the flute been around?

100 years?

Nope.

1,000 years?

Nuh-uh.

The flute is more than **40,000** years old.

That's older than your great-great-great-
a whole bunch of greats-great-grandparents!

No!

Yes!

The flute has a mouthpiece with a hole on the side rather than the top. The oddest thing about the flute is that you don't blow IN it. You blow ACROSS it, like when you make music by blowing across the top of an empty glass bottle.

It has a light sound, where each note seems to dance in the air after the last. It makes me think of a hummingbird flitting about, testing all the flowers, exploring the world.

Play for us, Ian!

The flute goes . . .

BOOM BOOM BOO

SAXOPHONES!

The saxophone is a baby in the instrument world.

Aldophe Sax

It was created in 1846 by Adolphe Sax, who grew up playing both the clarinet and flute.

Take a look at Melissa's shiny saxophone. Surely it's a brass instrument, right?

Nope!

It has a wooden reed, just like the clarinet.

You're looking at a WOODWIND!

It became popular with jazz musicians because of its smooth flow. The saxophone sounds the way a satin ribbon feels between your fingers.

BOOM BOOM
TROMBONE!

Originally called a **sackbut.**

Yes, fine, laugh, Rico.

Sackbut comes from a French word meaning

to *PULL* and *PUSH*

referring to the

LOOOONG

slide you move back and forth to make the notes.

The famous composer Beethoven was the very first person to use a trombone in one of his

BOOM
BOOM
BOOM BOOM

· Beethoven ·

TUBA!

THE LARGEST INSTRUMENT IN THE BAND. IT ALSO MAKES THE LOWEST NOTES! SO LOW THEY CAN MAKE YOUR STOMACH FEEL LIKE IT'S ON A ROLLER COASTER.

PLAY QUICKLY, CAROL!

Fantastic, Carol!

And now it's FINALLY time to talk about the drums. Felicity, please wait for my signal.

DRums

The drums are part of the percussion section, which also includes

bells, triangles, xylophones,

gongs, giant metal cymbals to crash

—basically anything you play by hitting it. You might use

a wooden stick, a mallet, or your hands.

Even the piano is a percussion instrument!

When you press **down** on the keys, they act as levers, popping up tiny mallets inside that strike thin or fat strings.

The thin ones make high notes.

The fat ones make low notes.

Drums are the oldest instrument in the world. Long before cell phones, people communicated with drums. When played on top of a hill, a drum's loud boom boom booms would travel for miles.

I guess I have to let you hear the drums . . . again . . . **sigh.**

The drums go . . .

Like I said. There's a perfect
instrument for everyone.

About the Band

The band members in this book were inspired by real-life musicians.

SIDNEY BECHET
(1887–1959)

Sidney Bechet was one of six born into a musical New Orleans family—his four brothers and his shoemaker father all played instruments. Sidney picked up the **CLARINET** at age six, but rather than reading music, he played by ear, making up his own flourishes and even creating new ways to hold the instrument to further improvise. While most jazz bands had trumpets on lead, Sidney often took the lead, improvising solos on the clarinet—something that had rarely been done before. The great Duke Ellington once said Sidney was "the very epitome of jazz."

VALAIDA SNOW
(1904–1956)

Louis Armstrong called Valaida Snow the "second best **TRUMPET** player in the world" (behind himself, of course). Everyone called her "Little Louis," but her skills were so incredible Armstrong should have been called "Little Val." Valaida also mastered the bass, banjo, cello, clarinet, harp, saxophone, and violin—all of which she played professionally—by age fifteen. She toured the world, wowing everyone with her talent, including Queen Wilhelmina of the Netherlands, who gave her a solid gold trumpet.

RUTH "WIDDY" GIPPS
(1921–1999)

One of the most prolific British composers in history, Widdy Gipps was a child prodigy, playing piano professionally by age four and winning songwriting awards by age eight. At sixteen she entered the Royal College of Music, where she fell in love with the **OBOE**. Later in life, frustrated with the discrimination against female composers, she started the London Repertoire Orchestra, which performed her own works as well as new works from other underappreciated living composers.

IAN ANDERSON
(1947–)

Born in Scotland, Ian Anderson started the band Jethro Tull, which mixed folk music with hard rock. Ian sang and played guitar and the **FLUTE**, often while balancing on one leg and wearing a signature large overcoat. Jethro Tull became one of the biggest bands in the world, touring with Led Zeppelin and Jimi Hendrix. Ian was even made a member of the Most Excellent Order of the British Empire by the Queen.

MELISSA ALDANA
(1988–)

When Chilean Melissa Aldana was three, her father competed in the Thelonious Monk International Jazz Competition, the most prestigious award a jazz player can receive. The Aldanas had the **SAXOPHONE** in their DNA. Not only did her dad play, but her grandfather was a professional as well. By seven she was transcribing Charlie Parker by ear. In 2013, after nearly three decades of the Thelonious Monk competition's existence, Melissa became the first woman—and first South American—to win top prize.

EMMANUEL "RICO" RODRIGUEZ
(1934–2015)

Growing up in Jamaica, Rico Rodriguez wanted to play the saxophone, but there weren't enough instruments at his school to go around. As older students graduated, Rico tried whatever they left behind. Finally he got to hold the instrument he was destined for: the **TROMBONE**. Rico became one of the pioneers of "ska" with his band The Specials. In ska, brass instruments are the stars. In 2007 Rico was made a member of the Most Excellent Order of the British Empire.

CAROL JANTSCH
(1985–)

In 2006, Carol Jantsch beat 194 other tubists for the role of principal **TUBA** player in the Philadelphia Orchestra while still a senior at the University of Michigan. She was the youngest member of the orchestra and also the first female tuba player in any major symphony orchestra. Her band, Tubular, is the first of its kind—a tuba band that plays pop music. She also runs a nonprofit called Tubas for Good with a goal of providing "high-quality instruments to underserved students" in the Philadelphia area.

TOM VENABLE

(1955–)

Tom Venable started playing drums professionally at the age of twelve. By fifteen he was playing with members of the *Tonight Show*, Count Basie, and Frank Sinatra bands. He graduated from Manhattan School of Music, fell in love, moved to upstate New York, and had two daughters. He took a job as a **BAND DIRECTOR** for a local school, though he continued to play gigs every weekend in the city. Now retired, he still records songs, teaches drum lessons, substitute teaches for music classes, runs a small recording studio in the Hudson Valley, and continues to play gigs on the weekend, outplaying musicians half his age.

COLLEEN ANN FELICITY VENABLE

(1980–)

My drummer/band director father taught me to love music, how the instruments worked, and the history of the people who mastered them—many of whom are in this book. He encouraged me to find the perfect instrument, and after decades of playing—from clarinet to fingerpicking guitar—I finally chose: **WORDS**.

All writers use music. Words are notes—some staccato, some legato, stretching out into the next. Punctuation is the rests between measures. And collaboration is key: words and art mixing together.

LIAN CHO

(1995–)

Lian Cho grew up in a musical family. She played the violin and trumpet as a child; her sister plays the flute and guitar; her mother plays a digital organ; and her father plays many different instruments, including the guitar, harmonica, cello, flute, and Erhu, a traditional Chinese instrument with just two strings. Lian listens to music while she creates her **ARTWORK**, and it inspires how she experiments with color. Just like music, color has many different tones and variations that work in harmony to bring the pictures to life.